Mce

The Mud Monster

A humorous story
in a familiar setting

First published in 2007 by
Franklin Watts
338 Euston Road
London
NW1 3BH

Franklin Watts Australia
Level 17 / 207 Kent Street
Sydney
NSW 2000

A CIP catalogue record for this book is available
from the British Library.

ISBN 978 0 7496 7135 8 (hbk)
ISBN 978 0 7496 7695 7 (pbk)

Series Editor: Jackie Hamley
Series Advisors: Dr Barrie Wade, Dr Hilary Minns
Design: Peter Scoulding

Printed in China

Franklin Watts is a division of
Hachette Children's Books.

The Mud Monster

Written by
Rosemary Billam

Illustrated by
Martin Remphry

W
FRANKLIN WATTS
LONDON•SYDNEY

Rosemary Billam
"I'm sure I would be the last one to finish in a Fun Run, but I hope I would have as much fun as Greg!"

Martin Remphry
"I went on school cross-country runs, but I was so slow they were more like cross-country walks!"

Greg was running
in the Fun Run.

Greg ran up the hill.

6

He ran in the stream.

9

Greg fell into
a bush.

10

11

Then he ran through a field.

13

Greg climbed over the hedge.

He rolled down the hill ...

16

17

... and across the line.

The judge said: "I now give
the prize to ... who are you?"

20

"It's the Mud Monster!"
cried Greg's mum.

23

Notes for parents and teachers

READING CORNER has been structured to provide maximum support for new readers. The stories may be used by adults for sharing with young children. Primarily, however, the stories are designed for newly independent readers, whether they are reading these books in bed at night, or in the reading corner at school or in the library.

Starting to read alone can be a daunting prospect. READING CORNER helps by providing visual support and repeating words and phrases, while making reading enjoyable. These books will develop confidence in the new reader, and encourage a love of reading that will last a lifetime!

If you are reading this book with a child, here are a few tips:

1. Talk about the story before you start reading. Look at the cover and the title. What might the story be about? Why might the child like it?

2. Encourage the child to reread the story, and to retell the story in their own words, using the illustrations to remind them what has happened.

3. Discuss the story and see if the child can relate it to their own experience, or perhaps compare it to another story they know.

4. Give praise! Small mistakes need not always be corrected.

READING CORNER covers three grades of early reading ability, with three levels at each grade. Each level has a certain number of words per story, indicated by the number of bars on the spine of the book, to allow you to choose the right book for a young reader:

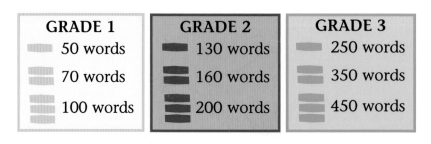

GRADE 1	GRADE 2	GRADE 3
50 words	130 words	250 words
70 words	160 words	350 words
100 words	200 words	450 words